THE FIELD BEYOND THE OUTFIELD

by Mark Teague

SCHOLASTIC
HARDCOVER

SCHOLASTIC INC.

New York

When Ludlow Grebe
began to complain
about the monsters
in his closet,

and the sharks
that swam by outside
every time it rained,

his parents decided
that he needed "something
real to think about."
   So they signed him up
to play baseball.

He was so far back
he was almost out of the outfield
and into another field altogether…

…where another
game of baseball
was in progress,
in a towering stadium
topped with pennants
and filled
with monsters
of various types.

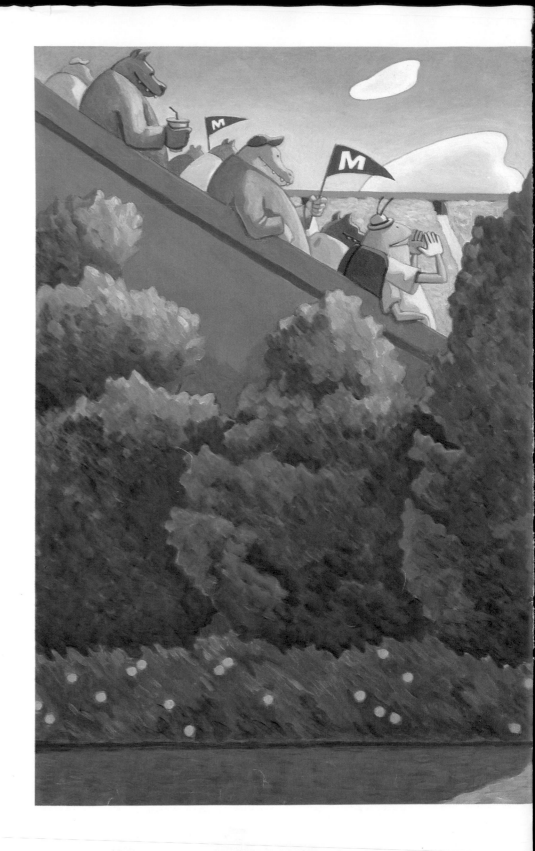

They told him to play back—
far, far back—to where the weeds
got scraggly and the other players
looked small as ants.

Ludlow put all of his energy
into learning the game.
He watched the pitches and
counted the strikes, and hardly
thought about monsters at all.

And when he finally
got a chance to play outfield
for the Oswald County Hornets,
Ludlow was ready.
A good ballplayer is always ready.

It was just what Ludlow
had feared might happen.
   But he reminded himself
that a good ballplayer must always
keep his mind on the game.
   So he watched the pitches and
counted the strikes,
and when the other fielder
asked if he could hit,
he told him that, in fact,
he could.

When the inning
changed, Ludlow
was whisked off
to try his luck
swinging the bat.

The monsters in the stands
became quiet when Ludlow
stepped up to the plate.
His stomach growled, and
his legs felt weak....

The pitcher threw
a fastball with one hand, and
a curveball with another...

So he did what all
good ballplayers do:
He tipped his hat
and tapped his shoes,
and grinned
a big-league grin.

...but Ludlow saw
the knuckleball coming,
and he swatted it
out of the park.

It seemed
like the cheering
would never stop.

That night Ludlow went
to bed without complaining,
and the monsters in his closet
didn't bother him at all.

He was ready for what
the next day would bring.
A good ballplayer
is always ready.

But Ludlow had his own game
to get back to, and night was coming on.

His parents smiled at him
when he came in from the field.
    "You'll get more action next time,"
said his father.

For Sarah *and*
Johnny

Library of Congress Cataloging-in-Publication Data

Teague, Mark.
The field beyond the outfield / by Mark Teague.
p.   cm.
Summary: When Ludlow begins to play baseball to help combat his
fears, he is placed so far out in the outfield that he becomes
involved with an adjacent game in which
a most astonishing thing happens.
[1. Fear—Fiction.   2. Baseball—Fiction.]   I. Title.
PZ7.T2193825Fi   1991
[E]—dc20   91-18055
CIP
AC
ISBN 0-590-45173-1
12 11 10 9 8 7 6 5 4 3 2   3 4 5 6 7/9

Printed in the U.S.A.   36

First Scholastic printing, April 1992

Designed by Claire B. Counihan

The artwork in this book was
painted with acrylic
on paper.